RIVER PARADE

ALEXANDRA DAY

RIVER

PARADE

VIKING

ACKNOWLEDGMENTS

My special thanks to Tom and Nathan Adams
for their patient cooperation, and to
Rabindranath Darling and Theodore Andrews
for their toy-making help.   —A.D.

VIKING
Published by the Penguin Group
Viking Penguin, a division of Penguin Books USA Inc.,
40 West 23rd Street, New York, New York 10010, U.S.A.
Penguin Books Ltd, 27 Wrights Lane, London W8 5TZ, England
Penguin Books Australia Ltd, Ringwood, Victoria, Australia
Penguin Books Canada Ltd, 2801 John Street, Markham, Ontario, Canada L3R 1B4
Penguin Books (N.Z.) Ltd, 182-190 Wairau Road, Auckland 10, New Zealand

Penguin Books Ltd, Registered Offices: Harmondsworth, Middlesex, England

First published in 1990 by Viking Penguin, a division of Penguin Books USA Inc.

1   2   3   4   5   6   7   8   9   10
Copyright © Alexandra Day, 1990

Library of Congress Cataloging in Publication Data
Day, Alexandra.   River parade / Alexandra Day.   p.   cm.
     Summary: When a young boy goes for a boat ride on the river and accidentally falls in,
he finds that swimming is not as frightening as he expected.
     ISBN 0-670-82946-3
     [1. Swimming—Fiction.   2. Boats and boating—Fiction.]   I. Title.
     PZ7.D32915RI 1990
[E]—dc20   89-48759

Printed in Japan
Set in Baker Signet

One afternoon it was so hot that all I felt like doing was watching the fan. Then my father said, "Let's go for a boat ride on the river." I said, "Okay, as long as I don't fall in."

I got Laurel, Upstairs, and Buoyant.

We drove to the river.

Dad helped me put on a jacket that would float.

The river was bigger than I thought it would be.

The boat was nice.
I liked the smell and the sound of the river.

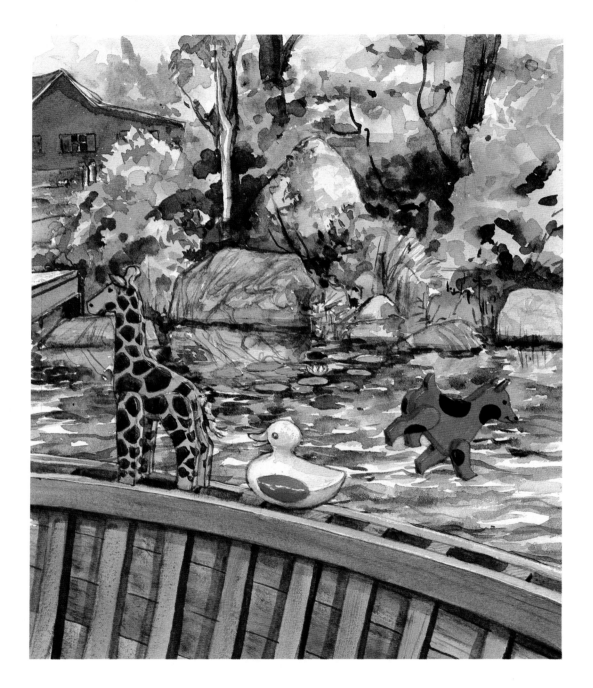

All of a sudden, Laurel fell in.
I yelled out, but he liked it.

Dad put a string on him.

I looked down at the fish.
They looked up at me.

I knocked Buoyant into the water,
and he liked it, too.

Dad tied him to the string.
Now I had two.

The river got narrow and noisy.

All of a sudden Upstairs jumped in.

We grabbed him just in time
and added him to the string
when the water got calm.

I reached over to move a branch
and then I was in, too.

It was cold and nice.
We were like a parade.
It's wonderful to swim
in the river,

as long as you're on a string.